Will Kostakis is an award-winning author for young adults. His first novel, *Loathing Lola*, was released when he was just nineteen, and his second, *The First Third*, won the 2014 Gold Inky Award. It was also shortlisted for the Children's Book Council of Australia Book of the Year and Australian Prime Minister's Literary Awards. *The Sidekicks* was his third novel for young adults, and his American debut. Will's fourth novel, *Monuments*, was the first in a fantasy duology and a Children's Book Council of Australia Notable Book 2020. The sequel, *Rebel Gods*, was published in 2020. As a high school student, Will won *Sydney Morning Herald* Young Writer of the Year for a collection of short stories.

The Greatest Hit

Will Kostakis

LOTHIAN

A Lothian Children's Book
Published in Australia and New Zealand in 2020
by Hachette Australia
(an imprint of Hachette Australia Pty Limited)
Level 17, 207 Kent Street, Sydney NSW 2000
www.hachettechildrens.com.au

A catalogue record for this
book is available from the
National Library of Australia

ISBN: 978 0 7336 4546 4 (paperback)

Cover design by Alissa Dinallo
Author photograph courtesy of Dion Nucifora
Typeset in Adobe Garamond Pro by Kirby Jones
Printed and bound in Great Britain by Clays Ltd, Elcograf S.p.A.

FOR TOBIAS VICKERS AND THE MUSIC WE MAKE

A Song

I used to love introducing myself. At the beginning of every year in primary school, whoever our teacher was at the time would make us introduce ourselves with a fun fact. I would always come up with something new. Others would recycle the same line year after year or waltz into class prepared for it. I wouldn't. Whatever my fun fact, I came up with it in that room, on that day. I wouldn't even let myself consider mine until others started reeling off theirs. It was exciting. Dangerous. There was the risk that somebody would say what I was planning to, and I would have to think up something new. But they never did. I used to love introducing myself. And I was exceptional at it.

We weren't asked for fun facts in high school. I figured we were too old. Then, come my first uni tute, Introduction to Media Studies, the practice was revived.

The ceiling fan rattled like it was two spins away from coming apart. The desks were arranged in a rectangle, so people were either staring at the stranger sitting opposite or pretending to be intensely fascinated by their fingernails. I was doing neither. I was watching people introduce themselves, excitement building as the distance between me and the speaker shortened. It felt like it had in primary school. Granted, the fun facts weren't half as interesting. They started off strong (Jasmine knew pi to forty decimal places and didn't hesitate to prove it), but as soon as somebody mentioned their professional goal (Quentin, a job in PR), that's all people shared. Copywriter. Newsreader. Editor.

When my turn came, I sat up taller. 'I'm Tessa and at my first job, I made a burger for a member of the British royal family.'

Mine was definitely the best fun fact. Not that it was a competition or anything, but people stopped pretending their fingernails were fascinating. The eyes of the room were on me. The guy beside me didn't speak. At first, I figured everybody wanted details – how far the British royal was from the crown, what their special demands were, if an imposing man wearing an earpiece watched me prepare the burger, that sort of thing. I started rambling, but stopped myself when I heard someone ask their friend if I was the chick who …

My heart sank. Nobody cared about my fun fact. The tutor's lips curled into an encouraging smile. I knew what he wanted to hear. I cleared my throat and caved. 'Oh and, um, a clip of me went viral a few years—'

Quentin was singing now. 'I love him, I love him, I love him, him, him.'

I grimaced. 'That's the one.'

Jasmine squinted at me until … a glimmer of recognition. 'Yeah, it is you. Same red hair.'

I should have dyed it. Shaved it. Assumed a new name. Moved to another continent.

I used to love introducing myself … before I was the 'I Love Him' girl.

While everyone else my age was taking their bold first steps into adulthood, I was just trying to outrun a song that went viral when I was fourteen. Every time I thought I had, somebody like Quentin was there to remind me I hadn't.

I didn't even try in my second tute, The Medieval Imaginary. When we were asked to introduce ourselves, I gave the people what they wanted.

I was Tessa. The 'I Love Him' girl.

If I couldn't outrun the song, I was going all in. When the Quentin of the group (Laila) sang a few bars, I joined her. I shouldn't have enjoyed it as much as I did.

My third tute, Introduction to Film Studies, would have gone the same way had the door not opened before I shared my fun fact.

'Sorry, sorry.' Her voice was melodic, but rough around the edges. It was an instrument I'd heard before.

My head snapped in her direction. Charlie. Only, she wasn't the Charlie I remembered. The bush of frizzy hair that once grew to her waist had been chopped and tamed. A neat blonde bob framed her face. She wore a faded T-shirt, artfully tattered jeans and ankle boots. My chest was in a vice, tightening and tightening as she claimed the vacant seat beside Amber (fun fact: aspiring journalist).

Charlie was here. In Melbourne. In my Introduction to Film Studies tute.

A voice to my immediate left. 'Hi, I'm Dylan. I'm in a band with my dad and granddad. We do gigs at the local pub.'

That made Charlie look up. She noticed me. I swallowed. It was like I had daggers lodged in my throat.

I felt the room's attention shift to me.

I cleared my throat harshly. 'Hi, um, I'm Tessa. I …'

Charlie's gaze bore into my soul. Her expression was blank, but I couldn't help reading into it … Shock … Anger … Whatever she felt, I knew I couldn't be the 'I Love Him' girl. Not in this tute. Not with her here.

I turned to Dylan and stammered a laugh. 'I … think I've been to that pub, actually.'

It was a terrible fun fact. It deserved to tank and it did. There was an awkward moment when the tutor expected more, and then she gestured to my right. Charlie's eyes were still on me, and just as Ava began to introduce herself, Charlie asked, 'Don't I know you?'

Ava went quiet.

There was a hint of mischief in Charlie's smile.

Amber gasped, putting it together. 'Yes! You had that song! Was it two years ago?'

'Four,' Charlie said, without breaking eye contact.

Amber began the chorus. When she hit the first *him*, Charlie scrunched up her nose at me. There were a few nods of recognition around the room before the tutor encouraged Ava to resume her introduction. Seven fun facts later, Charlie was asked to introduce herself.

'Charlie,' she said flatly, turning away from me.

I knew hundreds of fun facts about her and was curious which one she'd choose.

'I had a song written about me once.'

A Kiss

It was Amber's suggestion that the class head to the rooftop bar afterwards. I would have preferred the food court – I never end up planted opposite a scratched-up bathroom mirror making pufferfish faces at myself after a sandwich and lemonade combo – but Charlie was going, and the prospect of being that close to her again made my heart flutter. So I risked Pufferfish Tessa.

Amber offered to buy me a drink. I'd encountered people like her before. People who were a little too excited to meet someone who was internet-famous for, like, five seconds. I told her I would have whatever she did. I'd learnt it was easier to accept the drink, knowing full well that I was signing up for a long-winded conversation about things I hardly understood. People assume I have a grasp on the mechanics of going viral. But I don't. Not really. It just happened to me. Then it died down. And now I'm living in the echo.

The only free table at the rooftop bar was unnecessarily tall, so the ten of us had to sit on equally unnecessarily tall stools to reach. Charlie and I were on opposite ends. I wasn't staring. It was really difficult not to stare. Amber sat on my right. She talked my ear off, pausing only to sip her cider. And I snuck glances across the table. Charlie was bantering with some guy. If she snuck glances at me, I never caught her. I understood why she wouldn't.

*

I met Charlie on the first day of Year Nine. I was starting at a new school, so I met everyone on the first day of Year Nine, but I met Charlie especially. She was the only other St Maria's girl on the bus home. I sat beside her and did that annoying thing where I asked about the book she was reading while she was trying to read it, but Charlie wasn't bothered. She aimed the front cover at me. I said it looked interesting, and she asked if I wanted to read it. Before I could answer, she offered it to me.

'Like, to keep?' I asked, a little puzzled.

'No.' Charlie was a firm speaker, even back then. She was used to getting her way. She said it was because she was an only child, but she could've been the middle child of seven and still got everything she wanted. She was *adamant*, all the time. 'It's a loan. We'll do a trade. You give me a book, I give you this, and when you're done with it, I give yours back.'

I hadn't visited the St Maria's library yet, but I riffled through my bag on the off-chance a book had randomly materialised in it anyway. One hadn't. The bag only contained what I needed for homework that night. Oh, and a hardbound journal. I had ignored that it was a day planner and instead filled it with poems I discovered and some of my own. I had never shown it to anyone before. The journal was a present from my aunt two Christmases ago. I had kept it secret ever since, and I wasn't about to hand it over to somebody I didn't know.

I racked my brain for an excuse to delay the swap while Charlie watched, ready to surrender a book she was part way through … She was only *part way* through. 'Don't you want to finish the book before you give it to me?' I asked.

'No. And not because it's bad; I'm enjoying it a lot.'

'Then you should finish it.'

She rolled her eyes like someone who was hoping she wouldn't have to spell it out. I blinked at her. She had to spell it out.

'I was the new girl last year,' she said. 'Tons of people speak to you on your first day. You head home thinking you might be popular, and two hours later, you're convinced they only spoke to you because they had to. You don't want to be the weird new girl, so the next day, you don't approach anyone. But if I lend you my book, you have a reason to.'

I bit back a smile. Charlie might have overestimated how many people spoke to me on my first day, but in an instant, she had made changing schools feel less daunting. I wasn't going to reject her offer just because the only book I had to trade for hers was my most prized possession. I pushed past the fear and surrendered the journal. I expected it to make me feel sick, but it didn't. Like my body was telling me that I could trust her.

She handed me her book and as I flicked through it, I asked if someone had done the same for her on her first day. She said they hadn't, but she wished they had.

'You wrote the lyrics, didn't you?' Amber asked, ripping me off that bus and back onto my unnecessarily tall stool.

'Yeah.'

'Were you always a writer?'

I snuck a glance at Charlie. She was still bantering with the guy. I didn't know his name. He introduced himself when I was too distracted to listen or care. He looked like a Simon. He would be a Simon until proven otherwise. Charlie was looking at Simon in that intense way she used to look at me when she was really enjoying the vibe of a conversation. And I *was* staring now. I forced my eyes back to Amber. It took me a second to remember her question. Was I always a writer?

'Um, not really. But I loved it once I found it.'

'Songs?' Amber asked.

'Poems to start.'

I didn't begin to understand the appeal of poetry until we moved into the rental in Daylesford. There were two rhyming couplets painted on the back wall. Acrostically, the poem spelt out a word Dad didn't want me reading – like I hadn't heard him say it thousands of times, especially in the tumultuous months prior. My parents had sold our home and split their assets, Mum had run off, and Dad took out his frustrations on a poem that – aside from the word it spelt acrostically – was actually super sweet. It was a love poem, and even though I had never felt anything like what it described, it was a sucker punch to the heart. Come to think of it, that was probably the real reason he got rid of it. He was still feeling raw.

As the poem disappeared behind streaks of grey paint, I committed it to memory and later scrawled it in the back of the journal my aunt bought me for Christmas.

I had been notoriously hobby-less until that point. I had tried a lot, took a liking to few, and stuck with nothing. But that poem lit a fire in me. I collected more. Then I wrote my own. I stuck with it. I experimented. Haikus. Cinquains. Sonnets. I put my life in every line. I wanted to preserve it as I lived it because I knew the universe was like Dad with a bucket of grey paint. A few streaks and everything was gone.

Home. Mum.

The streaks came at the end of the year. Dad got the job in the city. We moved into the first place he applied for, an apartment in Preston.

I guarded that journal fiercely. I reread my haikus, cinquains, sonnets and was slingshotted back to Daylesford. I put my new life into new lines too, in case there came a time I wanted to be slingshotted back to Preston.

And I handed all that life to a stranger on a bus.

I ignored my homework and started the book Charlie gave me the moment I got home. I was about a quarter through it when she DMed me a link to a song. I plugged my earphones into my school laptop and pressed play. I heard a backing track tapped on a table, a simple repeated melody, and then singing. Charlie singing. Her voice was full, a little scratchy when she stretched it too high, and it was so beautiful that I didn't immediately recognise the words. *My* words. Charlie had taken my poem, the one about throwing paper planes off the balcony on a windy day, and turned it into a song. Two verses and a chorus that repeated. I listened to it all night.

I gulped my cider. My brain froze. I winced.

'Sorry, if I'm bombarding you with questions ...'

I waved Amber off, assured her it was fine.

'I can't be the only person who's interested in—' She gasped. Her eyes widened. 'I could pitch a feature to *Studiosum Diurna*.'

I only understood three quarters of that sentence and she could tell.

'The student paper,' she clarified. 'The feature could explore what happened to you and people like you, and reveal what you're all up to now.

A retrospective. "The Five Most Forgettable Internet Celebrities of the Decade So Far". Not that you're forgettable, but that'd be the tone. Light, fun, tongue-in-cheek.'

I glanced at Charlie. She was acting like Simon was the only person on the rooftop. I scowled.

Amber read into it. 'Probably not a good idea, you're right.'

I remembered the lunchtime we spent in the Music classroom when Charlie planted herself at the piano and started singing my words to different melodies. She encouraged me to try my hand at writing song lyrics, but I liked it when she took one of my poems and picked the chorus for herself. She could make the most ordinary lines sound special. The sunlight leaking through the frosted windows hit her frizzy hair just right. She had a halo.

I wondered what it would be like to press my lips against hers.

A loud thump. The waifish guy who was setting up the karaoke equipment raised one palm as if to apologise for interrupting everybody's conversations. He stood the speaker upright and pushed it towards the edge of the makeshift stage.

'You should go sing your song,' Amber urged.

'I …' I glanced again. This time, my eyes met Charlie's. Her expression was blank, a different blank to before. Maybe it was wishful thinking, maybe it was cider, but I couldn't help reading softness in it. She reached for her drink and returned her attention to Simon. 'I probably shouldn't.'

'You *should*,' Amber insisted.

A couple of others at the table echoed the sentiment, and the peer pressure might have worked if Charlie wasn't there, but I held my ground until somebody else took the stage. They were halfway through a tortured rendition of somebody's greatest hit and I was halfway through my cider when Ross (fun fact: mature age student) asked if anybody wanted another round. Whoever was after an excuse to leave took it. I kept mum. My night was tethered to Charlie's. If she stayed, I would. I thumbed the edge of my glass and waited for her to speak, heart thumping. She would be aware that the fewer of us there were, the less likely it was that she could avoid interacting with me.

When Charlie said she would love a cider, I told Ross I would too. I tried to sound nonchalant.

I thought I saw her lips twitch.

With half of our group bailing, it made no sense to spread across the entire table, so Amber encouraged Simon and Charlie closer. Turned out, Simon's name was Harry. He commandeered the spot to my left, but he didn't last long. As soon as his drink was done, he was off. He mumbled an excuse, but, honestly, I wasn't listening.

Charlie had ignored two chances to depart when someone else did, and unless she was super eager to chat to Ross and Amber, I was the reason. I mean, it obviously wasn't the quality of the live entertainment.

I held out hope that once Harry was gone, Charlie would take his seat and move closer. She didn't. She asked Ross what it was like to restart his studies in his thirties, and I wanted to shoo Ross and Amber away. I wanted to ask Charlie when she came back, what she'd been up to.

I wanted to apologise.

I still had the dregs of my first cider and all of my second to finish when she rocked her empty glass and indicated that it was somebody's turn to buy the next round. I volunteered. I was painfully aware of my posture as I walked to the bar. I checked over my shoulder when I arrived, hoping I would catch her. But she wasn't watching.

The woman behind the counter asked what I was having.

I didn't tell Charlie about my crush when it surfaced. My new life in Melbourne was flimsy as it was, I didn't want to risk making things worse. I spent my breaks between classes with her and her friends. And I was petrified that wrapping words around how I felt would jeopardise that. But then, when Charlie's friends were distracted by their extracurriculars or off on excursions and it was just the two of us … my crush was overwhelming, like I couldn't breathe and feel what I felt for her at the same time.

As the school term stretched on, I searched for hints that she liked me. Well, not just liked me, but felt so much, so intensely, that her lungs had trouble expanding when she was around me.

One lunchtime, it was just the two of us and she had enough cash to buy a canteen brownie for us to split. I broke off a piece. She told me she liked girls. I almost choked. My heart pounded.

'Me too.'

She slid closer until our arms touched. And I knew.

I bought drinks for everybody else. Carrying three full schooners was harder than it looked. When I returned, we were sharing the table with four guys in lab coats.

'Pub crawl,' Amber explained.

'Ah.'

A fifth guy asked about Harry's vacant stool. Emboldened by my one glass of cider, I told him he could take mine, and I swooped beside Charlie. I didn't tempt fate by looking at her, though. Her hand was inches from mine, our legs almost brushing together.

My breathing was ragged. I kept as still as possible, in case the slightest flinch scared her.

'So, what degree are you doing?' Charlie asked.

It took me a second to realise she was talking to me. I didn't know whether to cry, spew or scream. I swallowed hard. Daggers. 'Media and Communications.'

A beat. 'Arts.'

A shiver spread from the small of my back. It was my turn to say something, but what? Compliment her hair? Ask if her jeans were that torn to start with?

I had so much to tell her, but I couldn't just let it all spill out. I didn't want to scare her off now that she was so close. So close … I considered gently grazing the back of her hand as I reached for my glass. I didn't. I clasped the schooner, downed as much of my second cider as I could manage before my brain froze. I set down the glass and blinked at the condensation like it was the most interesting thing in the world. A deep breath. I had to tell her I missed her, and the longer I sat there, the harder it would be to suppress.

Would she actually want to hear how I felt?

I had to find out. I abandoned the rest of my drink and told the table I was leaving. I wasn't really. I was giving Charlie the chance to follow me. If she did …

I walked to the rooftop bathroom. Slowly. I waited by the sink. I waited. I waited. I made pufferfish faces at myself in the scratched-up mirror.

I pictured her standing against the sink beside mine, all tattered jeans and confidence.

I remembered her standing against the sink beside mine, in the boxy school uniform that did nobody any favours. She'd followed me to the bathroom. It was recess on the final day of term. They'd brought the holidays forward. It felt like the last time we'd be alone in the same room together. Her hand grazed mine. My eyes traced a line from our hands to her face. My heart beat like it never had before. We nervously inched closer.

We kissed.

I blew my cheeks out. She had asked what I was studying. I wondered if she was being polite or if ...

The bathroom door whined on its hinges. I pulled back from the scratched-up mirror.

Charlie stood there, bolt upright for one second, two seconds, three … Her shoulders dropped. Her expression softened. 'Hi.'

The door closed slowly behind her. We were alone in the same room together for the first time in an eternity.

I swallowed hard. Daggers again. She had followed me.

And suddenly, telling her how much I missed her didn't seem like enough. I needed to show her.

I took a cautious step towards her. I leaned closer in hesitant bursts. My lips found hers.

A kiss.

A miss.

She pulled back. 'No,' she said, short of breath. 'Tessa, you broke my heart.'

Awake

That night, I climbed into bed knowing full well that I wouldn't get much sleep.

I kept replaying history over and over in my mind.

The world stopped after our first kiss.

As it turned out, the onset of the most devastating pandemic in a century was the worst time to kiss the girl I liked because I was then locked in my apartment with only four reasons to leave – to shop, exercise, go to the doctor, work or study. Technically it was five reasons, but they kept counting the final two as one.

I only ventured outside for morning walks with Dad that always ended with us staring at empty supermarket shelves. Our apartment in Preston was a *between places* place, somewhere temporary while Dad settled into his new job. My aunt said it looked cramped in the photos on the real estate agent's website. I didn't think its size was a bad thing when we moved in. It meant I was never far from the fridge. Then I couldn't leave to kiss the girl I liked, because that wasn't one of the sanctioned reasons, and the apartment felt like a cage.

Dad didn't want me cooped up in my bedroom, so I spent my holidays lying on the couch, neck craned in an awkward position, laptop on my stomach, earphones in. Charlie and I would text each other before we started streaming something, so our experiences were synced. Some days we were great at it. Others, she would text *OMG!* a solid ten seconds before anything OMG-worthy happened. Usually kisses. One time, when a couple was really giving it their all in a torrential downpour, she asked how I felt about rain kisses. I hadn't thought about them enough to develop any strong feelings either way. Charlie had. She imagined the actors were damp and cold. I told her I thought rain kisses were romantic.

Noted, she texted, along with two emoji: a kiss and pouring rain.

I smiled at the screen, then Dad cleared his throat and I remembered he was in the room. It was weird having those conversations so close to him. He had claimed the dining table as his home office. I couldn't see it under the mountain of folders. He spent his days trying to sort them and taking important calls in his bedroom.

I was texting the girl I'd kissed, and he didn't know.

Dad cleaned twice a month. Whether we were in a house or a tiny apartment, he would turn the whole place upside down and use products that smelt so strong I questioned their legality. There was an unspoken agreement: he would do all the cleaning and I wouldn't complain about the music he blasted from the living room speakers while he did it. We had diverging tastes. He liked to say his was good and mine was bad. I disagreed, but he was scouring sinks and I was tolerating his playlist. I didn't have it too rough.

There was a song that would come on every so often. It was familiar. I must have heard it heaps as a kid, but Dad didn't let it play long enough for me remember it properly. Two ominous piano chords and the twang of a guitar, and no matter how engrossed in his cleaning, he would bark an order for his phone to skip the track.

It had come on one afternoon when Dad was dusting the skirting boards in the Daylesford rental. I was close enough to the phone to clock the song's details before it skipped. I snuck off to the bathroom for a listen. Piano chords. Guitar twang. A gruff voice, like the bloke who sang it had stepped into the recording booth after years lost in the woods.

It didn't sound any worse than the other songs Dad didn't skip.

Then the bloke sang about the woman he loved. Jodi.

I paused the track. A deep breath. I sat on the edge of the bathtub and blinked at the music streaming app on my phone for I don't know how long.

That was why Dad always skipped it. The song was about a woman with Mum's name.

He would skip the reminder of the woman who broke his heart.

I loved introducing myself, but there was one part of myself I hadn't introduced to him. I had known I like-liked girls for ages, since we'd pass pages torn from magazines around my Year Six classroom. While the others went gooey over a teen heartthrob's candid beach photos, I would sneak glances at the ad on the back – for makeup, eye cream, shampoo. I would trace over the contours of the model's face. I didn't tell Dad. I didn't tell anyone. Then Mum ran off with Stacey, the manager of the café down the street, and I *couldn't* tell Dad.

I was going to wait until uni, when I had a job and could move out.

It was a secret, but it wasn't a painful one. I knew I like-liked girls, but hadn't met one I like-liked. Then Charlie sang my words at me and I was a goner.

*

Charlie asked me if I'd written anything new as regularly as she asked me how I was. I sensed she wanted me to say that I was finally working on lyrics. I would type random lines and hoped they read enough like poems-in-progress that they threw her off the scent.

I was working on lyrics.

Charlie invited me to her family's Seder. It was usually a quiet affair, just her and her parents. Most of her extended family lived in Brisbane, with some members scattered across Europe. That made coming together in the past virtually impossible. It only took a pandemic for them to realise it was possible virtually. Charlie was in charge of sending out the invitations to the videoconference. I thought her family would think it was weird some random girl was intruding on their Passover tradition, but Charlie had a plan for that. I sat on my bed, my microphone muted, my camera off and my username set to Elijah. Everyone who noticed the prophet's presence laughed. The family divvied up the steps of the ritual. Every time Charlie spoke, I was transfixed, and every time she peered into the camera, I imagined she was looking right at me.

When school started up again, we learnt from home. Dad set up a makeshift study spot for me in the living room. It was the ironing board and a dining chair, but I appreciated the effort.

School was rows of tiny squares on my computer screen – windows into everybody's private worlds. I was jealous of the girls who lived in big houses and could broadcast from studies, or close to huge windows looking out into backyards. I was desperate to sprawl on a lawn, feel the dew on my back and stare up at the sky. I would have still been the pandemic's prisoner, but it would have been enough to trick myself into thinking I wasn't.

Charlie was only in one of my classes. Twice a week, I would ignore the tessellation of colourful squares that filled my screen, and zero in on hers. Teachers had rapidly developed a sixth sense for noticing when students had other windows open or were using phones they'd hidden from view, but we had a system. When Charlie scratched her forehead, it meant she'd sent me a message. I would minimise the class videoconference long enough to respond. I then scratched my forehead, so she knew there was a reply waiting for her.

I watched while she read what I sent her. Her internet connection was a little dodgy, so she was more pixelated than the other girls, but I could always tell when I made her smile.

*

I would call her during our breaks if Dad was in his bedroom.

One afternoon, I was on the living room floor, my phone off to the side. Charlie's voice, amplified by the loudspeaker, asked, 'Has it occurred to you that we're living through history?'

I thought about it for a second. 'Aren't we always living through history?'

'But this is *history*. Like, kids will write essays about this in school. Filmmakers will make heart-wrenching movies set in this moment for decades.' A beat. 'Do you ever worry that if they made a movie about you, it might be boring?'

'Our movies are supposed to be boring,' I said. 'We're supposed to stay home.'

I turned onto my side and imagined lying opposite her, smiling at her. I wanted to tell her *our* movie wouldn't be boring. It would be a heart-exploding love story.

'What's the first thing you want to do when we're not living through *history* anymore?' I asked.

She clicked her tongue against her teeth. 'Kiss you, weather permitting.'

I laughed. 'If it's not raining, we can always drape a hose over your clothesline.'

She laughed. I loved making her laugh.

I would have given anything to be able to reach through the phone and grab her hand.

Dad reappeared and I told her I had to go. I scrambled to end the call.

'Who was that?' he asked.

'Charlie.'

He knew her as the girl from the bus who lent me her book. He asked how she was.

Charlie didn't mind the abrupt ends to our chats. She didn't know about Mum and

Dad, the tumultuous months and the song he skipped when he was cleaning. She thought the chats ended abruptly because Dad was busy working from home and the conversations bothered him. Her parents were doctors at the Alfred, so she had her house to herself during the day. She would send me video clips of her glorious unsupervised life. They mostly captured her singing loudly as she slid across the kitchen tiles in her socks. In one of the clips, she asked me to be her girlfriend.

I said yes.

I should have told her everything, but I only said yes.

I groaned. My stomach was knotted. Cider mixed with regret.

I regretted not telling Charlie the truth.

I regretted not telling Dad I had a girlfriend.

I regretted the song.

I regretted trying to kiss her in the bathroom of the rooftop bar.

I wanted some way to fix everything. I still had her number. Whenever I transferred my contacts to a new phone, hers was the one I always checked was still there. Just in case.

I considered texting, apologising for the kiss, the song, but all the apologies in the world couldn't match the bigness of my stuff up.

I wrote a song. I didn't tell her I was working on it because I wanted to perfect it first. It was going to be my greatest hit. I eventually performed it for her. I sang and tapped a melody with my hands and everything.

She beamed when I hit the chorus.

'I love her, I love her, I love her, her, her.'

The next time she heard the song was when it was inescapable. It was the feel-good content everybody needed. Only it didn't make her feel good. It wasn't the version she'd heard. Whatever I did to make up for that needed to be bigger than a texted apology.

A Grand Plan

I had only attended two Introduction to Media Studies lectures. It shouldn't come as a surprise that I didn't know everything about the media.

The night of the botched kiss and me replaying history, I went to sleep having devised a grand plan. I was going to wake up early, waltz into the offices of the most popular newspaper in Melbourne and pitch an interview.

Yeah, the media doesn't work like that. I didn't get past security.

A Significantly Less Grand Plan

Studiosum Diurna wasn't the most popular newspaper in Melbourne, and featuring as one of the five most forgettable internet celebrities of the decade so far wasn't the perfect way for me to share my truth, but it was better than nothing.

It was my chance to right a wrong.

I had hoped to catch Amber before our Friday lecture, but she was early ... and speaking animatedly to Charlie. Like any self-respecting person, I hid behind a vending machine until everybody began filing into the theatre. I popped back into view and Amber gave me a little wave. She was still in the corridor, phone now pressed to one ear. She was speaking Greek, possibly Italian. Everything about her body language said it was a family call. Somebody couldn't get the TV to work and she had to pause her life to troubleshoot from afar, that sort of family call. She rolled her eyes. I waited with her, thinking it wouldn't take long. She'd get the TV working, we'd lock in a time for our chat, and settle into our lecture a couple of minutes late. Well, the call took twenty, and when I mentioned wanting to do the forgettable celebrities feature—

'Awesome,' she said. 'Let's do it.'

'Okay.'

Amber made a start for the building exit, and I realised she meant *now*. I was already uneasy about missing a third of the lecture. She wanted me to skip it entirely.

'I ...'

Charlie. I could skip one lecture they were going to make available online anyway for Charlie.

'Sure.'

She suggested the rooftop bar; I suggested the library. The greater the distance between me and cider, the better.

We found two chairs in a quiet spot. Amber said she would only need to ask a handful of questions, so I had to cram everything into a handful of answers.

Her pen was poised to take notes, but she recorded the conversation as a safeguard. 'Ready when you are,' she said.

I was as ready as I would ever be.

'I know not everything is autobiographical,' she began, 'but ... is there a guy this song wouldn't exist without?'

*

On the first Saturday of the lockdown, I nestled myself in the corner of the balcony that always made me feel the most creative. I had my back against the wall and my feet on either side of a potted aloe vera plant. My journal was open to a fresh double page. I ignored the printed lines and scrawled whatever I wanted, wherever. There was no real flow, but there was a subject that kept cropping up: Charlie.

I had resisted up until then, but she must have worn me down because I scribbled *ABABCB* in the corner of the page and started to reorganise the words into a different shape.

Sitting at the Music classroom piano, the sunlight hitting her hair just right, Charlie explained the structure of a typical song: verse, chorus, verse, chorus, bridge, chorus.

'ABABCB.' She punctuated it with a flourish of notes.

I frowned. 'Shouldn't it be VCVCBC?'

She smiled. 'You'd think.'

After I had two verses, a chorus and a placeholder for the bridge, I checked the balcony door was shut and tried singing. Another case of diverging tastes – I hated my voice and Dad loved it. He said it was haunting and beautiful. I always thought it sounded thin and fragile, but it worked for the song, which wasn't awful. I marked little asterisks whenever I hit a bit I didn't like, but on the whole, I was pretty happy with it for a first go.

'Who sings that?' a voice that was too high-pitched to be Dad's asked. It came from below. A balcony downstairs, probably.

I froze.

'Hello?' the voice asked.

'Me,' I answered. 'I sing it.'

There was a groan. 'I meant, who's the artist?'

'I wrote it.'

'Oh.'

I pushed myself up and peered over the barrier.

The speaker was on the balcony below our next-door neighbour's. He was tall and slender, and wearing a school sports uniform that probably fit him better before a recent growth spurt. I recognised the St Basil's College crest on his chest. I was useless at guessing how old boys were, but I guessed anyway: he was my age, maybe a year older.

I hesitated. I wanted to ask a question, but I was afraid of an honest answer. 'Did you … think it sounded professional?' I asked.

He smirked. 'Not the way you sang it.'

I considered tossing the aloe vera plant at him. 'Why are you in uniform anyway?'

He shrugged. 'What does it matter what we wear anymore?'

It was a fair point. He introduced himself without me asking. 'Dane.'

'Tessa.'

He squinted up at me and asked if I wrote many songs. I shook my head. He was on a music scholarship. He was, to use his words, a viola prodigy. He offered to help. He could teach me everything he knew about songwriting. I was enthusiastic. He said that it would cost me.

I seriously considered tossing the aloe vera plant at him.

Mrs Harris was taking us through the answers to the previous night's homework when I thought I heard my name. I turned down the volume and I *definitely* heard my name. I switched off my camera and stepped out onto the balcony. I leaned over the barrier.

Dane was in a wearable blanket shaped like a unicorn. 'Oh, thank God,' he gasped.

'Don't you have school?' I asked.

'I faked connection issues,' he said. He had one leg crossed in front of the other. He was bouncing on his heels. 'Do you have toilet paper?'

I nodded. Dad lucked out and scored a value pack the last time they restocked shelves.

'Can I have a roll?' he asked.

I told him it would cost him.

Dane encouraged me to fake connection issues to get out of class, but a system of secret face scratches was about as rebellious as I got. We scheduled our first songwriting session for that afternoon. Some teachers praise and reassure, gently inspiring their students to be better. Dane was not one of those teachers.

'Your melody is rubbish,' he said flatly.

'Thanks.'

'And your song doesn't feel like it's written *for* anyone.'

'It is, though.'

He shrugged. 'It's too vague. You were rattling off a list of general things you liked about her, but honestly, you could have been talking about anyone. Pick two moments with her, one for each verse, write about them in detail. Then come back to me, and we'll hang the words on a melody.'

We workshopped the song for weeks.

'So, there was no special guy who stole your heart?' Amber asked.

'No special guy.' I took a deep breath, expecting a wave of nerves to overcome me. But none did. I was Tessa, revealing another fun fact. 'The song was originally called "I Love Her".'

A Performance

I didn't have long. Ten minutes, max. Dad was out fetching pizza and I was planted at my ironing board, eyes glued to my laptop screen. Charlie missed my first video call.

And my second.

She answered my third. She apologised. She mentioned a conversation with her parents about Brisbane that went on and on ... but I didn't let her finish because we didn't have long. I started tapping my accompaniment on the ironing board.

'What are you doing?' she asked, right before I started singing.

She smiled and it was distracting. I closed my eyes and focused on keeping my taps consistent.

I sang about us sneaking into the Music classroom at lunchtime, I sang about the way my words sounded special when she put them to a melody, I sang, 'I love her, I love her, I love her, her, her.'

I sang about our first kiss in the bathroom, I sang about the way my heart thumped in my chest, I sang, 'I love her, I love her, I love her, her, her.'

I hit the bridge, and one line in, Dad asked what I was doing.

I panicked. I snapped the laptop shut and turned around. Dad was clearing space on the dining table for the pizza box. He had one eyebrow cocked, and his lips curled into a smile. 'Were you singing?'

I felt the fear as a lump in my throat. I swallowed hard. It didn't budge. 'Yeah,' I croaked.

I wondered how much of the song he'd heard. I sang that I loved *her* …

Dad set down the box and opened it. The apartment instantly smelt different. He asked whose song it was.

I knew I had to be honest, tell him that it was mine, that I wrote it for my girlfriend, Charlie.

I found some courage. 'I wrote it.' My voice wavered.

He asked if it was for school, and my courage evaporated.

'Yeah. It's a Music assignment.'

'Cool.' He didn't appear it give it much more thought than that. He motioned towards my usual seat.

I felt relief, but it wasn't like any relief I'd felt before. It was heavy, uncomfortable, sad.

My phone vibrated during dinner. I checked it, smearing pizza grease across the back. Charlie said she loved the song. She punctuated the sentence with a heart. She meant for it to make me feel good, but it made the heavy, uncomfortable sadness worse.

Tossing the crust of his final slice into the box, Dad asked to hear the song. I told him it wasn't ready yet, but the truth was, I wasn't ready yet.

He encouraged me. He said what he'd heard of the song sounded amazing. The more he persisted, the more unavoidable singing for him seemed. And it dawned on me that if I made slight changes to the lyrics, I could get by without reminding him of the woman who broke his heart.

'Okay.'

He reached for his phone. He wanted to record the song for my aunt.

I tapped the intro on the edge of the dining table. I closed my eyes. It was like I was strapped to the front of a train, checking the track as we sped over it. Before we passed a *she*, I adjusted it.

I sang about the boy who performed my poems for me, the light hitting his hair just right. I sang that I loved him, I loved him, I loved him, him, him.

My skin tingled, but I pushed on.

I sang about the boy who kissed me in the bathroom. I sang that I loved him, I loved him, I loved him, him, him.

I reached the bridge. Charlie hadn't heard this part ... about lying on the floor, hearing ~~her~~ his voice through the phone, wishing I could bridge the space between us. I stammered. I thought Dad might clue in. As far as he knew,

I only spoke to Charlie on the floor. I opened my eyes. He was beaming, nodding along. I sang the final chorus.

'That was so beautiful, Tessa.'

The knot in my stomach was painful. I smiled through it.

Amber sat back in her chair. Her notepad slid off her lap. 'And that was the clip that went viral,' she said.

I nodded, remembered she was only recording audio, and said, 'Yeah. Dad uploaded it for my aunt to see, but he set it to public and she shared it, and it must have been a quiet night on the internet because ...'

Charlie and I would text in bed until one of us got caught or dozed off. That night, she brought up Brisbane again. Her parents had applied for special permission to cross the Queensland border. They wanted to move closer to their extended family.

I told them no, she texted, along with two emoji: a kiss and pouring rain.

I replied with the same two emoji.

When my eyelids were heavy, and I was seconds away from falling asleep, my phone vibrated. An image from Charlie. It was a screenshot of Dad's video appearing on her feed.

I was part way through texting her not to watch it when she asked, *You cut me out?*

She didn't reply to my texts. The next day was worse. The video was everywhere. Dad had taken it down, but accounts with massive followings were reposting it, encouraging people to tag their #isocrush.

*

Dane stepped out onto his balcony with a block of chocolate. He went to call out my name and realised I was already there. He broke off a piece for himself and lobbed the block up to me. I caught it … *just*. It was the fancy type – the block was thin and flat, as if the company was hesitant to give people too much of a good thing. I helped myself to a whole row.

'She said anything?' Dane asked.

He read into my silence. I broke off another row and he didn't ask for the block back.

'Should have changed the pronoun to *you*,' he said.

I was drowning in *should haves*.

I sent dozens of unanswered texts before we shared another class. It had been days, and I had felt every agonising second. I logged in early. I searched the tessellation of squares on my computer screen as everybody joined the call. When I found Charlie, my heart almost leapt out of my chest. I minimised the window long enough to send her a message. I scratched my forehead and she didn't even flinch.

Somebody whistled the tune of 'I Love Him'.

I searched for her every time we shared a class, twice a week, until the day she didn't show up. I feared the worst and somebody who heard from one of her friends confirmed it. She'd moved to Brisbane.

People whistled my song in class. I thought of her every time and it stung.

Await

I was preoccupied at dinner. Dad caught me staring blankly at the wall behind him and asked where my mind was.

My mind was everywhere. In the library, telling the truth to Amber. At that same dining table, singing the altered song for Dad. On the floor, wishing I could reach through the phone and grab Charlie's hand while she spoke to me.

I found my voice. 'Charlie is in one of my uni classes.'

Dad's forehead creased. The name was familiar. He took a moment to comb through his memories, and then he nodded. It was one of those long, slow nods that told me he understood. Not just who Charlie was, but why having her in one of my uni classes was significant.

Dad took the video down the second time I asked him.

The first, he told me it was a beautiful song and everybody liked it.

'Not *everybody*,' I insisted. 'I don't like it.'

He launched into a supportive parent pep talk. He managed eight words before I blurted it out. All of it. I didn't like the song because it was a lie. I wrote it for Charlie. I changed the version I sang for him because I was scared.

'So please,' I added, 'can you take it down?'

He reached for his phone, avoiding my gaze while he deleted the post with a series of firm taps of the screen. I dreaded the moment he put his phone down.

He put his phone down. His eyes met mine. He asked me why I didn't tell him.

'I didn't want to remind you of Mum.'

He sputtered a laugh. It wasn't the reaction I expected. He took a deep breath and reset his face. 'You're her carbon copy, Tessa. I can't look at you without being reminded of her.'

I thought of him barking at his phone whenever that track came on. 'That doesn't make you angry? Like the song you always skip because it has Mum's name in it?'

Dad's eyes widened. 'You noticed?'

'You're not subtle. But I get it, she broke your heart.'

He told me that wasn't what made him angry, and then he sat back. Another deep breath. He squinted, as if the words he was after were *just* out of sight. 'I liked being married to your mother. A lot,' he added. 'I shared my life with her, and I thought I knew her completely. I didn't see she was hurting. She was hiding a part of herself to keep me happy and I didn't notice. *That* makes me angry. Somebody I cared about suffered because of me. And if I'd caught on, maybe it would've been different. It wouldn't have got to the point where she needed to run away. Maybe.' He squinted some more. I waited for the words. 'I don't want you to hide a part of yourself to keep me happy. You being happy makes me happy. Get me?'

I nodded. 'I get you.'

I told him about our shared tute and the cider session. I neglected to mention the attempted kiss in the bathroom. He didn't understand why, after waiting so long, I was going through *Studiosum Diurna* and not speaking to her directly.

'It needs to be big.'

'Does it?' he asked.

*

Studiosum Diurna published every fortnight, so it was an excruciating five-day wait between my interview and the launch at the rooftop bar. Amber invited me once she heard the feature made the cut. It took me hours to build up the courage to invite Charlie.

It was a short, boring text, but my breath caught in my throat while I typed it. *Delivered* became *Read* and a shiver spread from the small of my back. I watched the screen until my eyes watered.

No reply.

I thought very hard about what to wear to the launch. I even considered cutting some holes in my jeans. I went so far as to grab the scissors from the kitchen drawer before I reconsidered.

*

It was one of those nights where the sky was blanketed with clouds that threatened a downpour at any moment, but the rooftop was packed regardless. I couldn't tell if it was Wednesday-night busy or launch busy.

I had imagined canapés and speeches, but apparently a launch just meant they dropped a couple of stacks around the rooftop and the contributors and editors who were available celebrated with a drink.

I searched the crowd. There was no sign of Charlie, but there were a few people with their heads buried in the student paper. I forged a path towards the closest stack by the makeshift stage.

I helped myself to a copy. I almost missed Amber's feature on my first flick through. I had five days to imagine it, a double-page spread devoted to my journey, complete with photos. I had forwarded several. The reality was a little different.

A lot different, actually.

The bottom third of page sixteen was devoted to 'The Five Most Forgettable Internet Celebrities of the Decade So Far'. We each had a square that featured a photo and barely any text.

THEN: Tessa was a fourteen-year-old whose viral song, 'I Love Him', was inescapable for a week after proving popular with Boomers.

NOW: Tessa is studying a Bachelor of Arts (Media and Communications) and a lesbian. Turns out, 'I Love Him' was originally written about a girl!

There had to be more. I checked page seventeen. Nothing but a crossword.

I looked up and spotted Amber immediately. I cleared the distance between us. She was happier to see me than I was to see her.

'Oh, hey!' She had to shout over everybody else.

I shook the scrunched-up issue at her. My heart hurt. 'I thought it was going to be longer.'

'Yeah, the editors—'

A loud thump. Our eyes snapped to the stage. The waifish guy who was setting up the karaoke equipment held up an apologetic palm before standing the speaker upright.

I turned back to Amber.

She restarted. 'The editors cut it down a lot to fit in the space, which I didn't anticipate. That was a bummer,' she explained, her expression souring for all of three seconds. '*But* whether it's ten lines or fifty, I've still had my first feature published, which is pretty cool.'

I was lost for words. I had wasted five days, five days of being in the same city as Charlie, thinking I had prepared this grand gesture, and all I had managed was a fifth of a third of a page, and most of that was a photo. And not even one I supplied. A screenshot of the video that went viral.

My phone vibrated in my jeans pocket. I pulled it out, glanced at the screen and forgot how to breathe. One new message from Charlie. *Here.*

I searched the crowd again and I caught sight of her. Her lipstick matched her T-shirt. She was scanning the rooftop until a whine of feedback pulled her focus. She watched as the guy fixed the microphone to its stand.

'I loved interviewing you,' Amber said. 'I think I might rework the piece and publish it on my website, if you're okay with that?'

If I waited for the rework, there was no guarantee it would turn out how I hoped. I didn't want to look back on this moment weighed down by *should haves*. I had to step up.

'Did you feel that?' Amber asked. 'I think it's starting to rain.'

I didn't answer her.

The guy preparing for karaoke retreated and pointed at the microphone. It was ready for whoever wanted it. People swarmed around the display of the karaoke machine, agonising over which artist's greatest hit to butcher. I cleared a path to the stage and took up the microphone.

'Hi.'

The whine of feedback. The whine of the people swarming the display. It was their turn.

I waited for Charlie's eyes to find mine, and that was long enough.

'My name is Tessa, and this is my greatest hit.'

ALSO BY WILL KOSTAKIS

 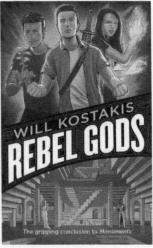

'page-turning adventure fiction
peppered with humour, romance and
high-stakes dramatic reversals'
Sydney Morning Herald

If you would like to find out more about
Hachette Children's Books, our authors, upcoming events
and new releases you can visit our website,
Facebook or follow us on Twitter:

hachettechildrens.com.au
twitter.com/HCBoz
facebook.com/hcboz

THIS BOOK BELONGS TO

~~~~~~~~~~~~~~~~~~~~~~~~~~~~~~~

I celebrated Australia Reads 2020 with this brilliant book
from my local bookseller and Hachette Australia.

TAKE THE TIME.

This book has been specifically written and published to celebrate Australia Reads.
Australia Reads is a unique cross-industry campaign to promote the benefits of reading
to all Australians. It is supported by: Australian Booksellers Association (ABA), the
Australian Library and Information Association (ALIA), the ALIA Australian Public
Library Alliance (APLA), the Australian Society of Authors (ASA), the Australian
Publishers Association (APA), the Australian Government, through the Office for the
Arts, and the Copyright Agency's Cultural Fund.

#australiareads #takethetime

australiareads.org.au